Why Is It Raining?

Especially for my sister, Peggy Ribbons,
and for Sarah and Tom Henderson

Why Is It Raining?

Jan Godfrey
Illustrated by D'reen Neeves

Augsburg 🔥
MINNEAPOLIS

Billy Bear woke up one morning and jumped out of bed.
It was raining. Splish. Splash.
Raindrops ran down the window pane.
"Why is it raining?" said Billy Bear to himself.
"Rain is very wet. When it rains I can't go out to play."

It rained and it rained and it rained.
Harder. Harder. Faster. Faster.
Splish. Splash. Splish. Splash.
The houses were wet. The gardens were wet.
The streets were wet. The cars were wet.
Everything was wet.

"Why is it raining?" Billy Bear asked his sister Bessie.
"I don't know," said Bessie Bear.
"But I shall use my new umbrella today.
It's very pretty."

"Why is it raining?" Billy Bear asked Mama Bear.
"I don't know," said Mama Bear.
"But I shall wear my raincoat today.
Go and bring your bike in out of the rain.
It's getting wet."

Outside, Billy Bear met Bertie Bear.
"Why is it raining?" asked Billy Bear.
"Don't know," said Bertie Bear.
"But look, I'm wearing my best new boots."
And he SPLASHED in a puddle.

"Why is it raining?" Billy asked Papa Bear.
"I don't know," said Papa Bear.
"But open the door, Billy Bear.
Here comes the postman."

"Why is it raining?" Billy Bear asked the postman.
"I don't know," said the postman.
"But I need my big waterproof hat today.
Now mind you don't drop that letter in a puddle."

The rain kept raining.
Harder. Harder. Faster. Faster.
Splish. Splash. Splish. Splash.
There were big dark clouds in the sky.

Billy Bear put on his raincoat and his hat and his boots
and went to see Grandma Bear.
The raindrops ran down his nose.
He jumped and splashed through the puddles
all the way to Grandma Bear's house.
It was fun.

"Why is it raining?" Billy Bear asked Grandma Bear.
And Grandma Bear helped Billy Bear to take off his raincoat
and his hat and his boots.
She sat Billy Bear on her lap.

"Now," said Grandma Bear. "That's a good question.
God sends the rain to grow plants and trees
and to give us enough to drink."

"Everybody needs the rain.
It keeps everything fresh and clean.
The birds like it. They like bathing in it.
The snails like it. They slime about in it.
Animals in hot countries like it. It makes them cool."
"I like it," said Billy Bear.
"But where does it come from?"

"The rain comes out of the clouds.
It falls on the mountains and the hills
and runs into little streams," said Grandma Bear.
"The little streams run into bigger streams
and then into rivers, all the way to the sea."
"All from a few drops of rain?" asked Billy Bear.
He thought God must be very clever.

"Can I have a glass of rain to drink?" asked Billy Bear.
"Let's have some of my home-made lemonade, instead,"
said Grandma Bear.

WHY IS IT RAINING?

First North American edition published 1994 by Augsburg Books
First published by Tamarind Books, in association with SU Publishing,
London, England

Copyright © 1993 AD Publishing Services Ltd
Text copyright © 1993 Jan Godfrey
Illustrations copyright © 1993 D'reen Neeves

ISBN 0-8066-2744-1   LCCN 94-070319

Manufactured in Singapore   AF 9-2744

98   97   96   95   94   1   2   3   4   5   6   7   8   9   10